S0-DOQ-443

GRANBY ELEMENTARY LIBRARY
7101 Newport Avenue
Norfolk, VA 23505

THE LEGEND OF
SLEEPY HOLLOW

Copyright © 1985, Raintree Publishers Limited Partnership

All rights reserved. No part of this book may be reproduced
or utilized in any form or by any means, electronic or mechanical,
including photocopying, recording, or by any information storage
and retrieval system, without permission in writing from the
Publisher. Inquiries should be addressed to Raintree Publishers,
310 W. Wisconsin Avenue, Milwaukee, Wisconsin 53203.

3 4 5 6 7 8 9 10 11   97 96 95 94 93 92 91 90 89

Library of Congress Number: 84-9931

Library of Congress Cataloging in Publication Data

Gleiter, Jan, 1947-
    The legend of Sleepy Hollow.

    Summary: A superstitious schoolmaster, in love with a wealthy
farmers' daughter, has a terrifying encounter with a headless
horseman in this tale of the Catskill Mountains.

    1. Children's stories, American.   [1. Ghosts—Fiction.
2. Catskill Mountains region (N.Y.)—Fiction]
I. Thompson, Kathleen.   II. Hockerman, Dennis, ill.
III. Irving, Washington, 1783-1859: Legend of Sleepy
Hollow.   IV. Title.
PZ7.G4817Le   1984   [Fic]   84-9931
ISBN 0-8172-2117-4 lib. bdg.
ISBN 0-8172-2260-X softcover

THE LEGEND OF
SLEEPY HOLLOW

Retold by Jan Gleiter
and Kathleen Thompson

Illustrated by Dennis Hockerman

Raintree Childrens Books
Milwaukee

Not far from the village of Tarry Town, there is a little valley in the high hills. A small brook runs through the valley, making a sound just soft enough to put a person to sleep. The whistle of a bird or the tapping of a woodpecker is almost the only noise ever heard. A dreamy feeling seems to hang over the land.

Some say that there is a spell on the valley. It is true that the good people there often see strange sights and hear music and voices in the air. The valley is called Sleepy Hollow.

In this peaceful spot, there lived for a while a man by the name of Ichabod Crane. He was a schoolteacher. And he looked more than a little like his name. Like a crane, he was tall but very thin. He had narrow shoulders, long arms and legs, and hands that stuck a mile out of his sleeves. His feet could have been used for shovels. His head was small and flat at the top, with huge ears, large, green, glassy eyes, and a long nose. It looked like a weather vane was sitting on his skinny neck to tell which way the wind blew.

I chabod kept a good school. He only whipped the strong children. He never whipped the weak ones. He even played with some of the bigger boys after school. And he sometimes walked the smaller ones home, but only if they had pretty, older sisters.

Ichabod Crane also gave singing lessons to the young people in the neighborhood. That's how he met Katrina Van Tassel. Katrina was the only child of a Dutch farmer. She was eighteen and plump as a partridge. She had cheeks as pink as one of her father's peaches. And she was not just pretty. She was rich.

When Ichabod went to see Katrina, he always looked at the farm first. His mouth watered. He didn't just see pigs. He saw every one of them with an apple in its mouth, ready to be cooked. All the pigeons were put to bed in a nice pie and tucked in with a blanket of crust. The geese were swimming in their own gravy. Every turkey that he saw was stuffed and wore a necklace of sausages. Ichabod Crane fell in love.

But there was another man who loved Katrina. His name was Brom Van Brunt. Brom was big. He was so big and so strong that everyone called him Brom Bones. Brom was good at all kinds of racing and fighting. But, rough as he was, he had a good heart.

Brom had four friends who went everywhere with him, playing tricks and having a good time. Whenever there was a loud noise in the night, people cried, "There goes Brom Bones and his gang!"

All of the men in the valley were afraid to talk to Katrina because of Brom Bones. Ichabod Crane was afraid, too. But he was smart. When he visited Katrina's house, he pretended to be giving her singing lessons. But he was really telling her how pretty she was.

Brom didn't like that. He wanted to fight with Ichabod. But Ichabod wouldn't fight with Brom. So Brom and his gang played tricks on the schoolteacher. They stopped up the chimney of his schoolhouse. So when he made a fire, the room filled with smoke. They broke in at night and turned the place upside down. And Brom taught his dog to "sing" like Ichabod.

Then, one day, Ichabod got a note inviting him to a party at Katrina's house. He let the children out of school early. Then he spent hours getting ready. Finally, he borrowed a horse from a farmer. He wanted to look like a brave knight when he rode up to the Van Tassel house.

The horse was an old workhorse. There wasn't much in him anymore except meanness. He was thin and shaggy, with a head like a hammer. His mane and tail were tangled and full of sticks. One eye was blind. The other had the look of the devil in it. His name was Gunpowder.

So Ichabod rode Gunpowder to the party. Brom Bones came, too, on his fine black horse, Daredevil.

Ichabod danced every dance with Katrina because he was such a good dancer. Brom Bones sat in a corner by himself.

When the dancing ended, people started telling stories—ghost stories. Ichabod listened to them all. And Ichabod believed them. That was one of the things about Ichabod Crane; he believed in ghosts.

Most of the stories were about a ghost who rode a horse across the valley—a ghost without a head. Everyone in Sleepy Hollow knew about the ghost, and some of them said that they had seen him. They said that he was a soldier whose head was carried away by a cannonball. His body, they said, was buried in the churchyard. The ghost rode out every night, looking for his head. In the morning, he rode back to the church. He was known, at all the country firesides, as the Headless Horseman of Sleepy Hollow.

It was a very witching time of night when
Ichabod started for home. All of the ghost
stories came into his head. The night grew darker
and darker. The stars seemed to go deeper into the
sky. Sometimes the clouds hid them from his sight.
Ichabod had never felt so alone.

Suddenly, he saw something huge and dark in the
shadows—huge and dark, and very, very scary.

As Gunpowder slowly moved closer, Ichabod saw
that the thing was a man on a black horse. As
Ichabod passed him, he started riding behind
Ichabod. But he did not speak. There was something
awful about his silence.

Suddenly, the moon came out from behind a cloud. Ichabod saw the man clearly. He had no head.

Ichabod kicked Gunpowder to make him go faster. Gunpowder dashed away, through thick and thin, stones flying and sparks flashing. Ichabod couldn't stop him. Ichabod's clothes flapped in the air. The headless rider stayed right behind them. His head was tucked under his arm.

All Ichabod could think of was getting to the churchyard. That was the ghost's home. Just before the church, there was a bridge. "If I can reach that bridge," he thought, "I am safe!" Just then he heard the black horse close behind him. He even thought that he felt the horse's hot breath.

Ichabod kicked Gunpowder, and they thundered over the bridge.

But they weren't safe yet. Ichabod looked back. The terrible ghost rider was standing in his saddle, just about to throw his head. He threw straight at Ichabod. Ichabod tried to duck, but it was too late. The horrible thing hit him with a crash. He fell to the ground. And Gunpowder, the black horse, and the ghost rider, went on like a high wind.

The next morning, the village people found Gunpowder at his owner's gate, quietly eating grass. The schoolteacher wasn't at school.

Later, they found Ichabod's black hat near the bridge. Close beside it was a pumpkin, all broken to pieces.

Some say that Ichabod was carried off by the
Headless Horseman. Some say that Ichabod left
the village in the night, went to school to learn the
law, and became a judge.

Brom Bones married Katrina and always laughed
when anyone talked about the pumpkin.

After that, there were even more stories about the
Headless Horseman. And people say that on some
nights they can hear Ichabod Crane singing in the
hills around Sleepy Hollow.

GRANBY ELEMENTARY LIBRARY
7101 Newport Avenue
Norfolk, VA 23505